First published by arsEdition in 1997.
Text copyright © Jutta Langreuter
Illustrations copyright © Andrea Hebrock

First published in the UK in 2001 by
Glowworm Books Ltd. Unit 7, Greendykes Industrial Estate,
Broxburn, West Lothian, EH52 6PG, Scotland

Telephone: 01506-857570
Fax: 01506-858100
E-mail: admin@glowwormbooks.co.uk
www.glowwormbooks.co.uk

ISBN 1 871512 73 5

Printed by Proost in Belgium

UK edition edited by Lindsey Fraser

Reprint code 10 9 8 7 6 5 4 3 2 1

Who's Your New Friend Roddy?

Told by Jutta Langreuter
With illustrations by Andrea Hebrock

Glowworm Books

When Roddy Rabbit came home for tea everybody
could see that he was very happy indeed.
'I have a new friend,' he announced.
'Really?' said Mummy Bunny Rabbit, slicing an onion.
'He's called Edgar, and we've been sailing boats on
the river,' Roddy told her.
'Splendid,' said Mummy Bunny Rabbit.
'And we built a dam,' said Roddy, proudly.
'Wonderful,' said Mummy Bunny Rabbit, passing the
cabbage for Daddy Bunny Rabbit to chop up.

'And we played flooding,' added
Roddy, grandly.
'Smashing,' said Beanie Bunny
Rabbit.
'And we're going to play together
again tomorrow,' said Roddy.

The next evening Roddy ran all the way home and arrived just in time for tea.

'Where have you been?' asked Daddy Bunny Rabbit, putting the salad on the table.

'Playing,' Roddy said, panting, 'playing with my new friend. We've had a great time.'

'What were you doing?' asked Beanie

'We built a secret tree cave.'

'I'm glad you've got a new friend,' said Mummy Bunny Rabbit, 'would you like to invite him for tea tomorrow?'

'Yes!' Roddy beamed.

'Good. I think I'll bake a carrot cake,' Mummy Bunny Rabbit said.

Roddy thought for a moment. 'He might not like carrot cake,' he said quietly.

'Of course he will,' laughed Mummy Bunny Rabbit, 'everybody loves my carrot cake!'

Daddy Bunny Rabbit found Beanie in a terrible state
when he arrived home the next evening. She was as
white as a sheet as she tried to tell him, 'Daddy….
Daddy… It's Roddy …..'
'What's happened to Roddy?' asked Daddy Bunny
Rabbit.
'Nothing's happened. It's just that he brought his
friend home,' whimpered Beanie. Then she began to
sob. 'He's a…a…he's a…'
Without waiting a moment longer, Daddy Bunny
Rabbit rushed into the house. But what he saw there
made him stop in his tracks. His fur stood up on end.

Roddy was sitting at the table with a fox! It was a
small fox, but it was a fox nevertheless. Both Roddy
and the fox were eating carrot cake.

Mummy Bunny Rabbit was standing behind Roddy
and she looked very, very frightened. She was holding
a huge soup ladle behind her back, just in case…

'Hello Daddy!' said Roddy cheerfully. 'Meet Edgar,
my new friend. He loves carrot cake.'

'Hello,' said Edgar, and he began to stand up.

'Just stay where you are,' said Daddy Bunny Rabbit
quickly.

'This carrot cake is absolutely delicious,' said Edgar.

'Would you like another slice?' offered Mummy
Bunny Rabbit nervously.

'Oh, yes please,' said Edgar.

'Mummy, why aren't you eating any?' asked Roddy.

'I think I'll have mine later,' she replied, giving them
both another slice, but never letting go of the ladle.

'And where's Beanie?' asked Roddy.

'Yes, I haven't met your sister,' said Edgar politely.

Daddy and Mummy Bunny Rabbit looked anxiously
at each other.

'Roddy,' said Mummy, 'when you've finished,
would you wash the cake tin for me please?'
'But Edgar and I want to…' began Roddy.
'That's all right,' said Edgar, 'I'll help you.'
'Roddy can wash up perfectly well on his own,'
said Daddy Bunny Rabbit from the doorway.
'Why don't you take another piece of carrot cake
home with you?' Mummy Bunny Rabbit suggested.
'Thanks very much, Mrs Bunny Rabbit,' said Edgar,
choosing a slice from the plate.
'See you soon…,' she said, still trembling with fear.
Edgar turned when he reached the door, 'Thanks
again,' he said.
'See you tomorrow!' called Roddy, smiling at his
friend.
But he wasn't smiling for long.

As soon as Edgar had gone, Beanie rushed indoors and flung herself on to the armchair, weeping. Mummy Bunny Rabbit leant, exhausted, against the kitchen dresser.

'What sort of friend is that?' Daddy Bunny Rabbit asked Roddy angrily. 'We don't make friends with our enemies.'

'Enemies?' asked Roddy. He didn't understand.

'Haven't you noticed? Your friend is a fox,' his father explained.

'Yes, but…'

'Edgar is a fox. And foxes eat rabbits.'

There was a loud sob from the armchair.

'No he won't!' said Roddy, furiously. 'He's my friend!'

'All foxes eat rabbits,' said Daddy Bunny Rabbit. 'It's a fact.'

'But Edgar isn't like that!' shouted Roddy.

Mummy Bunny Rabbit tried to help. 'Listen, Roddy…' she began.

But Roddy wouldn't listen. 'He isn't! He isn't! He isn't!' he insisted.

The next morning Edgar was sitting in the tree cave when Roddy arrived. He'd run all the way there. 'I can't stop,' he gasped, 'Beanie is trapped and I've got to get back to her straight away.'

'What happened?' asked Edgar.

'She was collecting eggs from the hens – we need lots of eggs for Easter. She was chatting away and began to tell them that you'd been in our house, eating carrot cake. They giggled and cackled so much that she didn't hear the farmer arriving with their feed. He threw it in and closed the door of their cage. Beanie got such a shock that she didn't move fast enough, so now she's locked in with the hens. The crows came to tell us.'

'All because of me,' sighed Edgar unhappily.
'Well it's not exactly your fault,' replied his friend.
'When did this happen?' asked Edgar.
'Yesterday evening,' wailed Roddy, 'everyone tried to chew at the wire fencing, taking it in turns all night. Me too! But it was no good. The hens tried. Even the cockerel tried. And Beanie is being really brave. But she might be stuck in there forever and ever!'

'Look,' said Edgar, and he bared his teeth at
Roddy. 'My teeth are sharper than yours.'
Roddy looked a little alarmed, but then he
understood. 'What a brilliant idea.
Hurry up then!' he shouted and
the two friends set off.

The rabbits and hens scattered when Edgar arrived. 'Calm down everyone,' said Roddy. 'Quiet!' He was very nervous. In fact everyone was nervous, except for Beanie, who was strangely calm. She was sitting in the cage, surrounded with goodies and titbits popped through the wire by the rabbits.
Edgar took a close look at the fencing. 'This wire is quite thin,' he told them, before biting at it several times. The other animals didn't move a muscle.
Except for Beanie. 'Here's a good place,' she pointed underneath the lock. 'Try here.'

The only sound to be heard was Edgar snipping away at the wire with his pointed teeth.

'It's not working,' observed Beanie.

Edgar stopped and thought for a little while. 'I think I'd better try something else,' he said. They could hardly watch while the fox panted and snapped, burrowed and wheezed.

But finally they heard Beanie say, 'Thank you Edgar!' She was out of the cage. At long last she was free. She was standing next to Edgar, whose nose was covered in earth. Next to them was a hole that he'd dug to help Beanie escape. The hens decided that they were really very happy where they were, so they stayed in the cage.

Later that day, the Bunny Rabbits arranged a huge party. And the guest of honour was Edgar. And of course there was plenty of delicious carrot cake.

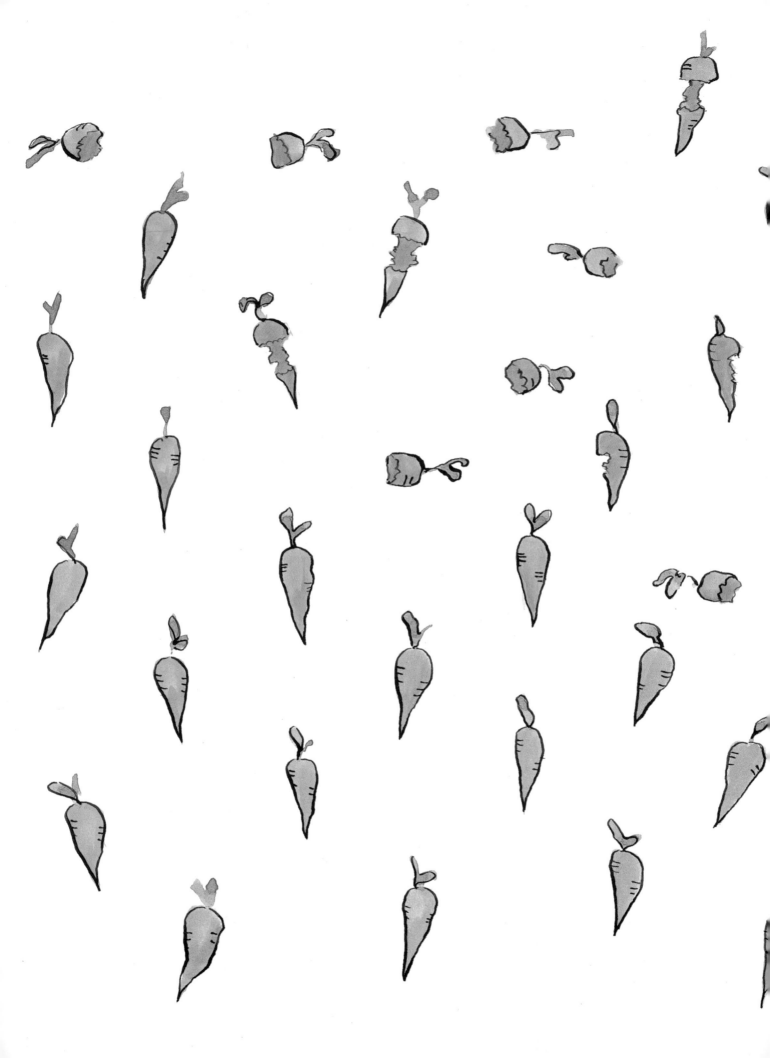